Wishing Well Will

Will

by

Alan Gibbons

First published in Great Britain in 2013
by Caboodle Books Ltd
Copyright © Alan Gibbons 2013

A Catalogue record for this book is available
from the British Library.

ISBN 978 0 9569482 4 3

Cover and Illustrations by Hunt Emmerson
Page Layout by Highlight Type Bureau Ltd
Printed by CPI Group (UK) Ltd.

The paper and board used in the paperback by
Caboodle Books Ltd are natural recyclable products
made from wood grown in sustainable forests.
The manufacturing processes conform to the environmental
regulations of the country of origin.

Caboodle Books Ltd
Riversdale, 8 Rivock Avenue, Steeton, BD20 6SA
www.authorsabroad.com